HEY YOU!

We need to ~~tork~~ talk. *(talk)*

Isn't it time you
stopped reading boring books
once and for all?

Well, ~~repeet~~ *repeat* after me:

From this
moment on,
I only read
books that are
100 percent
UNBORING
~~GARANTEED~~! *guaranteed*

Like this one!

OK, now that we've got that ~~strate~~ straight, you can go ahead and read this book.

I used all of my pocket money to sponsor it, so you know it's good!

And I'll be back soon with some very smart and ~~valyabel~~ advice.
valuable

Mitey Mikey
Life Coach for Kids
(and by the end of this book
that will include YOU!)

Mitey Mikey's segments were filmed in front of a live studio audience . . . in his backyard.

Join the So Wrong Book Club at
sowrongbooks.com

First published in 2019 by

Text copyright © Michael Wagner 2019
Illustrations copyright © Wayne Bryant 2019

The moral rights of the creators have been asserted.

National Library of Australia
Cataloguing-in-Publication data:

Wagner, Michael, 1964– author.
So wrong / Michael Wagner ; Wayne Bryant, illustrator
ISBN: 9780994251770 (POD)
For primary school age.
Advertising-Parenting-Parodies-Juvenile fiction.
Bryant, Wayne, 1974–, illustrator.
A823.4

Cover design by Wayne Bryant
Text design by Wayne Bryant and Michael Wagner
Typeset in many different fonts, short stories in Minion Pro

billygoatbooks.com

COMING UP

1

Dad and I love to play. Sometimes we wrestle. Sometimes we race. Sometimes we bump and shove and trick and do anything to win.

Except cheat. We don't cheat. We do everything but that.

We've been like this for years. I remember when it all started. It was way back when I was little.

I remember the day exactly. I can still see myself. I was a toddler, just a sweet little toddler.

It was a hot day. I was wearing a diaper. That's all, just a diaper. It was hanging down between my knees. It weighed a ton. It was packed to the rafters!

Dad was taking me for a walk. We needed some fresh air. My diaper had stunk the house out.

Diapers can do that. Diapers can be terrible. My diaper was a disaster that day.

But it wasn't my fault!

Mum and Dad were the ones who fed me. They should have fed me different things. Maybe things that smelled nice...

...like perfume.

And anyway, a smelly diaper is no big deal if someone – like, say, my dad – would have just changed it. But he wouldn't. No way!

If there was one thing my dad would NOT do it was change a diaper.

2

My dad is very useful at many things. He was even way back then.

He would feed the baby.

He would wash the baby.

He would burp the baby.

He would even clean up the baby's chuckies.

But he would not – I repeat, NOT – change anyone's diaper. Not even mine.

That's because Dad has a weak stomach. Certain smells make him feel sick. Certain diaper smells in particular.

He couldn't do it. Which was a problem because, that day, Mom was out. And that left just the four of us at home: me, Dad, our dog Tiger, and my sagging diaper – which, by then, had a personality of its own.

So what did Dad do?

He got us out of the house and into the fresh air. Great thinking, Dad!

You know, he's very, very, VERY smart . . .

. . . sometimes.

3

There we were walking down the street, me holding Dad's hand, and Tiger straining the lead in Dad's other hand.

All that fresh air completely drowned out the smell of my diaper. We didn't have a care in the world.

Until Dad said five little words. And those five words triggered something deep inside my tiny, toddler brain.

'Race you to the lamppost.'

That's all it was.
1)Race 2)you 3)to 4)the 5)lamppost.*

---

* Just so you know, lamppost can also be spelled lamp post. So it could have been six words. But the way Billy's dad said it that day, it was definitely five.

What should have happened next was a funny little toddle along the footpath. I should have been giggling and squealing and Dad should have been pretending to race me.

But, oh no, that's not how my toddler brain reacted to those five little words.

Not at all.

Inside my small, perfectly round head, a spark was set off. And that spark flew straight into a giant box of firecrackers.

My brain went *BANG!*
It exploded with an idea.
A big idea.
A powerful idea.

I had to beat Dad to the lamppost. I had to get there first.

Somehow, little Billy had to WIN!

MORE OF

THE DIAPER

AFTER THIS SHORT . . .

A letter from the Principal

Dear Prospective Student,

At Nude School we believe that learning should be experienced the way nature intended it – in all its glory.

That's why we expose our students to a world of opportunities by stripping down the educational process to its bare essentials. How else can students ever truly show everyone just what they're made of?

And because our pupils don't have to grapple with stuck buttons, knotted laces, dreaded zippers (that's a mistake you only make once, isn't it, boys!) or any other bothersome wardrobe malfunctions, they're free to focus on what really counts: raw learning and naked ambition.

So throw away that stuffy uniform and get comfortable just being yourself. Visit us at Nude School any time for a guided tour. You won't believe what you'll see!

Warmest wishes,

L Godiva

Ms L. Godiva

Principal,
Nude School

p.s. All classrooms are heated.

Science really heats up
in the prac lab!

at nude School

We love sports of all sorts.
We even have our own Olympics!

IT'S JUST LIKE ANCIENT ATHENS — ONLY NUDER!

Our orchestra is famous for its
legendary wind section.

at nude School

Every aspect of the human form
is on display in our Art classes.

And we're not afraid to use life models!

So what are you waiting for?

Join us today at . . .

And now for Part Two of

THE DIAPER

Previously on The Diaper:

Billy's diaper is as full as an elementary school hat rack and Dad won't change it. So, to get some fresh air, they've gone for a walk along the street. But when Dad suggests a race to the lamppost, a powerful idea is sparked in Billy's tiny mind.

4

My beady little toddler eyes spotted the lamppost. I can still see it there. It looked a million miles away.

I didn't start running straightaway. I just toddled along, giggling.

I wanted Dad to think it was all just a bit of fun. I knew I couldn't beat him with pure toddler speed.

I knew I had to trick him somehow.

Dad jogged alongside me, pretending to be running as hard as he could.

'You're going very fast, Billy,' he said. 'You're a speedy little guy.'

Dad was babying me! He thought I was going as fast as I could.

You'll see, I thought. I'll turn on the speed, soon enough...

...when the time is right.

I kept chuckling and bouncing along, until Tiger headed for a tree on the nature strip. He dragged the lead hard. Dad stumbled to one side.

This was my chance.

This was it.

I bolted!

I ran like the wind – a foul wind, because of my diaper.

I ran as fast as I could, but my diaper was holding me back. It was sagging between my legs.

Suddenly, Tiger was right beside me. I knew Dad was on the other end of that stretched-out lead.

He was catching up too!

The harder I ran, the more my diaper dropped.
I couldn't get up to full speed.
I could hardly run.
I had to skip sideways.

Suddenly, Dad was right beside me!

'Wow,' he said. 'You are speedy.' Then he grinned and added, 'But not as speedy as Daddy.'

He was right. How could I run as fast as him? My diaper was around my ankles. It was hanging so low it was dragging along the ground. I had to do something or I'd lose!

Then my brain did that sparking thing again.
I got another idea.
It was a great idea.
It was an awesome idea.
It was the best idea ever!

But it was going to be tough to pull off.

5

Without stopping, I took one foot out of my diaper.

I started swinging it around my ankle like a hula-hoop.

When it was up to full speed, I flicked the diaper off my foot.

I looked up. It was spinning through the air –
spinning, spinning, spinning.

It looked like a lumpy frisbee.

It spun right over Dad's head. It dropped in front of him. Dad staggered. He was about to get hit by a flying diaper.

And it was loaded!

The diaper landed on Dad's flip-flop. His foot got
caught in a leg-hole. He slipped and stumbled onto
the nature strip.

'Get it off!' he yelled. 'Please, someone get this
thing off!'

I ran to the lamppost.
I slapped it.
I was there first.
I'd won!
'Billy,' I said. 'Winner.'

6

I was only a toddler and I'd beaten my dad. I was thrilled. I was over the moon. I was so happy I didn't even care that I had no pants on.

What a day it was. The sky seemed extra blue, the sun felt extra warm and, without my diaper, the air smelled extra sweet.

But on our way home, Dad stopped and squinted at me.

'Billy,' he said, 'if you weren't just a sweet, innocent little toddler, I could have sworn you deliberately tripped me up with that overloaded diaper of yours.'

I grinned. I acted dumb. I clapped my hands together and said, 'Da-da. Diaper. Flip-flop!'

It was all an act – a baby act. I didn't want Dad to know how much I needed to win. That way I'd have a better chance of beating him the next time. And maybe even the time after that.

So that's how it all started – right back when I was little. And Dad and I have competed against each other every day since.

And I still win almost every time.

THE END

Hang on
a ~~minut!~~
minute

Sure, that diaper story was
sweet enough, but what
exactly did you learn?

And that's where I come in.

As you know, I'm Mitey Mikey,
Life Coach for Kids,
and I'm here to

TEACH YOU A LESSON
ONCE AND FOR ALL!

And trust me,
you have A LOT to learn.

So listen up!

In a moment I will give your first
free sample life lesson, but before that,
I have to explain just how much of an
expert I really am.

On the next page you will find a
scientific graph that explains how much
smarterer I am than you.

Prepare to be ~~astonished~~!
astonished

See how much smarter~~er~~ than you I am!

But don't feel discouraged because all that's about to change.

To be nearly as smart as me all you have to do is copy everything I do all of the time.

Which brings us to your first free sample life lesson.

Once you truly understand this lesson you will be well on your way to being almost as smart as me.

Good luck as you begin this exciting ~~jerney~~!
journey

What Mitey Mikey loves	What Mighty Mikey does NOT love
cakes	exploding cakes
crazy dangerous fun	getting blown up

Do Love	Do NOT love
more crazy dangerous fun because you haven't learned your lesson	going to hospital in an ambulance
free hospital food	free hospital needles

Do Love	Do NOT love
nurses	doctors
having fun with the other patients	other patients getting revenge

Do Love	Do NOT love
buttons you can push to get lots of attention	being lonely because you've pushed too many buttons
being stuck in hospital	being freeeeeeeee!

OK so the last two should be the other way round, but it's better this way, so

WHO CARES!

Now, if you thought that was great –
and I know you did –
wait till you see my next free
sample life lesson.

It will make you want to save all your pocket money and spend it on the best life coach for kids in the world –

ME!

But first we return to this book for another story that is nice and short and 100 percent unboring

GUARANTEED!

1

The moment the school bell rang, Timmy grabbed his brand-new soccer ball, ran out of the classroom, and raced to find his neighbor, Jaxson.

On the way to school that morning, Jaxson had promised to have a kick of the soccer ball with Timmy after school. Timmy had been looking forward to it all day.

As usual, Jaxson was with his three best friends: Knuckles, Dog-face and Hammer.

They were all big, tough sixth graders, and they looked scary, but Timmy wasn't afraid of them – not at all.

That wasn't because Timmy was especially brave for a five-year-old. He was no braver than you or me. He was just at that lovely age when you think everyone is nice – even big, tough, scary-looking, 12-year-olds.

So when Timmy spotted Jaxson and his friends, he sprinted over and excitedly tugged at his neighbor's sleeve.

'You can walk me home now, Jaxson,' Timmy said. 'And, look, the soccer ball Uncle Ben gave me is still brand new. I didn't let anyone kick it all day. That means we get to have the first kick. How cool is that?'

'Whatever,' grunted Jaxson.

Knuckles, Dog-Face and Hammer sniggered. Jaxson turned his back to Timmy. But Timmy didn't mind.

'We can have a kick as soon as we get home,' Timmy said. 'Dad made me a goal in the backyard. He tied a rope between two trees. We can take shots. Best of ten!'

'I didn't know you liked soccer,' Dog-Face said to Jaxson, with a smirk.

'So, Jaxson loves soccer now, does he?' joked Knuckles. 'Who knew?'

'Yeah, he's a real soccerhead,' Hammer said, high-fiving Dog-Face.

'I'm not a soccerhead!' said Jaxson, pointing at Timmy. 'He is!'

'Don't worry, Jaxson,' said Dog-Face, sarcastically, 'you're allowed to like any baby games you want . . . skipping . . . hopscotch . . . soccer.'

Jaxson's friend all laughed.

'Yay. That means we can both be soccerheads,' said Timmy, cheerfully.

'I HATE soccer!' snapped Jaxson. 'And I'll never be a stupid little soccerhead like you! Now go and wait at the gate!'

Timmy wandered over to the school gate where he clutched his shiny new soccer ball and waited for Jaxson to walk him home.

He waited . . .

and waited . . .

and waited.

Until finally Jaxson stormed past, grunting,
'Come on, you little soccerhead. Let's go.'

'Look,' said Timmy, holding up his soccer ball.
'Kobe wanted to have a kick with it at lunchtime,
but I said no. I told him the first kick was going
to be with you – that was our promise.'

Jaxson marched on.

2

'How good is soccer!' said Timmy, rushing to keep up with his neighbor as they walked home. 'I didn't used to like it, but now that I have a brand-new soccer ball, I LOVE it. It's the best game in the world. You love soccer too, don't you Jaxson?'

'Soccer's dumb!' said Jaxson. 'It's a dumb game played by dumb people. Like you!'

Jaxson turned on his heels and marched away. Timmy stood there thinking for a moment, then shook his head.

'I'm not very good at it either, Jaxson,' he said, rushing to catch up. 'Uncle Ben says you just have to practice until you get the hang of it! You'll see. Just come over to my place once you've had your afternoon snack. I bet you get good at it really fast.'

'That's NOT going to happen,' said Jaxson, walking even more quickly.

'But you promised,' said Timmy.

'Well I un-promise,' said Jaxson.

'There's no such thing as un-promising.'

'There is now,' said Jaxson.

Timmy frowned for a moment, then brightened up and said, 'Oh, I get it. No one can ever break a promise, so you're making a joke. Hahaha. That's a good one, Jaxson. You're so funny!'

Jaxson shook his head and kept moving.

'Uncle Ben says it's the BEST feeling ever,' said Timmy, jogging to keep up. 'That first kick of a new soccer ball. I didn't let anyone have a turn. I only took it out for Show and Tell.'

Jaxson drowned out Timmy's voice by loudly humming.

'And, guess what?' said Timmy raising his voice. 'I've just decided that you can have the very first kick ever. The first one!'

Jaxson hummed louder.

Timmy jogged alongside his humming neighbour.

'Oh, if you're worried about being the goalie,' Timmy yelled, 'we'll take turns. But just don't kick it too hard, okay? I'm not that good at goalkeeping yet.'

Jaxson's humming wasn't working, so he starting singing instead.

> 'Shut up, little soccerhead.
> Shut your little pie hole.
> Shut up, little soccerhead.
> Shut your little . . .'

'That reminds me!' shouted Timmy. 'Mom made me an apple pie for my afternoon snack. You can have some too. And if you come to my place, we'll be able to start playing soccer even sooner.'

Jaxson stopped and spun around.

'How many times do I have to tell you, you little soccerhead!?' he shouted. 'Soccer's dumb. You're dumb. And having to walk my embarrassing little neighbor home every day is TOTALLY dumb. Now stop pestering me! I'm NEVER going to play soccer with you EVER! GOT IT?!'

Jaxson stormed off. Timmy just stood there. He needed a moment to himself.

3

'It's okay, Jaxson,' sniffed Timmy as he caught up. 'I get in bad moods sometimes too – just ask Mom. One time I even karate chopped Dad's butt. But don't worry because I know the best cure for bad moods. It's called having a kick of a socc–'

'DON'T say it!' said Jaxson, cutting Timmy off. 'I don't want to hear that word again.'

'Oh, okay,' said Timmy. 'I won't say that word, but let's have ten shots at goal each and whoever scores the most is the winner.'

'ARGHHHH!' cried Jaxson, marching for a few steps before suddenly stopping.

'Hang on a minute,' he said, slowly turning around. 'Maybe I *will* play soccer with you after all. Except there's one small problem.'

'What?' asked Timmy, his face lighting up.

'We don't have a ball to play with,' said Jaxson.

'Yes, we do,' said Timmy, holding up his brand-new soccer ball. 'That's what I've been saying all along. It's right here. See?'

'Got it!' said Jaxson, snatching the ball out of Timmy's hands and wedging it under his arm. 'Now where's my . . .'

Jaxson dug around in his school bag before pulling out something sharp that Timmy had never seen before.

'Do you know what this is, Soccerhead?'

Timmy shook his head.

'It's a compass,' said Jaxson.

'Does it point north?' asked Timmy.

'It's not that sort of compass, moron. It's the sort of compass you use to draw perfect circles. AND to put holes in stupid, dumb, boring soccer balls.'

With that, Jaxson stuck the point of his compass into the skin of Timmy's soccer ball.

Air rushed out in a long sigh. The ball went from hard and round to soft and floppy.

'There,' said Jaxson, handing the ball back to Timmy. 'Now there's no way we can play soccer after school. No way at all. So build a bridge and get over it, Soccerhead!'

More of

after another . . .

iON HO

Tired of the **WEIRD WAYS** parents think?

Had enough of all THAT
ADULT STRANGENESS?

Well BRIGHTEN UP, kid,
because the clever folks at

would like you to meet your
new best friend . . .

AFTER

Only adults do chores, son. You go back to the home theater and I'll bring you a cold drink and some snacks before I get on with the gardening.

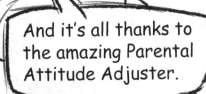

And it's all thanks to the amazing Parental Attitude Adjuster.

AFTER

Here's my credit card, darling. There's no limit, so take whatever you need. Go on, treat yourself. You deserve it!

Whoa! Thank YOU, Parental Attitude Adjuster!

Time now for Part Two of

Previously on Soccerhead:

Jaxson promised to play soccer with Timmy after school, but on the way home he's used his compass to poke a hole in Timmy's brand-new soccer ball. Talk about a meanie!

4

Timmy looked at his flat soccer ball. It wasn't shiny and new any more. It was lumpy and ruined. He used it to wipe away his tears as he quietly said, 'But you promised.'

'Now we're talking!' yelled Jaxson. 'At last there's something fun to do!'

Timmy looked up to see Jaxson standing at the edge of a giant square of freshly laid cement. It was grey and glistening.

'Watch this, Soccerhead!' Jaxson said. 'I'm going to jump right into the middle of that wet cement. That should make a good impression. Hahaha! Get it? A good IMPRESSION. Oh, forget it, you little soccerhead.'

As Jaxson paced out his run-up, Timmy said, 'But you'll ruin the cement.' Then he muttered, 'Like you ruined my soccer ball.'

'And that,' said Jaxson, 'is the difference between a nerdy little soccerhead like you and a cool twelve-year-old like me.'

Jaxson scraped his foot on the grass, marking the start of his run-up.

'Tough guys don't care about soccer balls or other little baby toys,' Jaxson continued. 'We look for excitement and danger. Now stand back and watch how the cool kids have fun.'

Timmy stepped backwards and held the flat soccer ball against his face. He was worried he'd get splashed by the wet cement.

Jaxson ran at the grey slab and launched himself like a long-jumper.

He landed in the very center of the slab. Wet cement rose up in a wave around his feet. But then the wave reversed, wrapping itself tightly around Jaxson's shoes.

'What a leap!' yelled Jaxson. 'I could make the Olympics. I'm gonna do that again.'

But when he tried to pull his feet out of the cement, he couldn't.

'Hang on,' he said. 'I'm stuck.'

5

'This cement weighs a ton!' said Jaxson. 'I can't move at all! What am I supposed to do now, Soccerhead?'

'That's easy,' said Timmy. 'Just undo your shoes and jump right out of them.'

'Yeah, obviously!' barked Jaxson, untying his shoelaces. 'I've got another pair of shoes at home anyway.'

He stepped out of his shoes and jumped.

When he landed he was still in the wet cement, and well short of the edge. And, once again, when he hit the grey concrete, another circular wave flared up before slapping right back down around his feet.

'I'm stuck again!' cried Jaxson.

'Don't worry,' said Timmy. 'Just take off your socks.'

'I was about to say that!' said Jackson, pushing both socks down as low as they could go. He slid his feet out and jumped.

Again, he landed short of the edge. Again, the wet cement grabbed him. But this time it had wrapped around his bare feet.

'Got any more bright ideas, Soccerhead?!' said Jaxson. 'I'm down to my feet!'

Timmy thought for a moment, then said, 'I know, take them off.'

'What are you talking about?!' cried Jaxson. 'How am I meant to take my feet off? What is WRONG with you, Soccerhead!? They're my feet! I can't just take them off!'

'But I've got an Allen key right here,' explained Timmy. 'I keep it on my keyring.'

'Why didn't you say so?' cried Jaxson. 'Quick, throw it over!'

Timmy unclipped the Allen key and tossed it to Jaxson. Jaxson reached out. He fumbled. The key was about to drop into the wet cement when he clutched it to his leg.

'Nice throw, Soccerhead,' he said. 'NOT!'

6

'All you have to do,' explained Timmy, 'is slide your ankles out of the way, and unscrew your foot-bolts.'

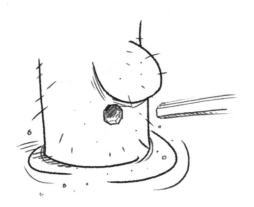

Jaxson unscrewed each foot-bolt until he heard them *click*.

Then he leapt right off his feet . . .

And landed on his leg-stumps.

The cement gripped his legs as tightly as a pair of grasping hands.

'You're kidding!' shouted Jaxson.

'Just undo your hip-bolts,' suggested Timmy.

'Thank you, Einstein,' Jaxson replied before unscrewing both hips.

He rocked back and forth, then heaved his upper-body right off his legs.

SPLOP!

He landed on his butt. The wet cement gripped it tight.

'This is really getting annoying!' Jaxson said. 'And before you say it, I know, just take off my butt and throw myself forward. Thanks for the tip, Brainiac!'

Jaxson undid his belly-button-bolt, releasing his bottom. He swung his arms as hard as he could and hurled his torso forward.

SPLOSH!

'This is getting ridiculous!'

'You're almost there,' said Timmy. 'Just take off your head.'

Jaxson undid his neck bolts. He tucked the Allen key into his shirt pocket and used both hands to lift off his head.

POP!

He tossed his head into the air. It landed on the grass at Timmy's feet.

FUMP!

'You did it!' said Timmy, dancing around. 'You got out of the cement!'

'Yeah, great,' said Jaxson. 'And how am I supposed to get home without a body?'

'I'll carry you,' said Timmy.

He picked up Jaxson's bag with one hand, then grabbed the flat soccer ball with his other hand, then realized, 'I don't have enough hands to pick you up as well!'

'That's perfect!' moaned Jaxson. 'This day just keeps getting better and better!'

'Hang on,' said Timmy. 'I know what to do. I'll kick your head home, just like a soccer ball.'

'What!?' said Jaxson.

Timmy had no choice. He booted Jaxson's head all the way home. It was the most fun he'd ever had with his big neighbor.

And from that day forward, Timmy was proud to say he LOVED soccer. In fact, he was proud to call himself a total soccerhead.

And Jaxson was a soccerhead too – in his own way.

THE END

YEAH, YEAH,

WHATEVER!

As if there aren't
WAY more important things in life
than playing soccer and
ending up just being a head!

I think you'd better . . .

Sometimes in life

you have to tell a nice little bedtime
story to a tiny baby.

goo
goo

ga
ga

And that's

BORING!

WAAAAAAH!

Unless you do it the Mitey Mikey way!

'But, Mitey Mikey,' I hear you say,
'how can anyone make a pefectly
normal and sweet bedtime story
unboring?'

I'm glad you asked
because THAT is the
subject of this . . .

Sample Life LESSON #2:

How to Make a Sweet
Little Bedtime Story
UNBORING.

If you study this
story closely
you will learn
more

than
you ever
thought possible
about being awesome
like me.

Here's how it happens

goo-goo ga-ga

TRANSLATION

Please tell me a bedtime story, big brother. PLEASE!

Sure thing, Sis. But NO TOUCHING MY SPELLING! Because doing that makes me feel dumb. And I can't be dumb, because I'm Mitey Mikey.

goo-ga

TRANSLATION

Deal!

And then, the reading begins.

The Veree Hungree Caterpooper

by Mitey Mikey

In the lite of the moon,
a littel egg lay
in a puddel of scum.

One Sunday morning the scum-puddel
got veree warm and
– Pop! –
out of the egg came a tinee and
veree hungry caterpooper.

The veree hungree caterpooper
looked for food.

He found some - a grate big, steeming
pile of it.

On Munday he
ate throogh one
crusty teebag,
but he was still
hungry.

On Tyoosday he ate throogh two
shiny blak banana skins, but he
woz still hungree.

On Wednsday he ate throogh
three fuzzy bitz of blue orange peel,
but he woz still hungree.

On Thersday he ate throogh four
soggy piza crusts,
but he woz still hungree.

On Friday he ate throogh fyve things
that wer cheezy, but wer not cheeze,
and he woz still hungree.

On Saterday he reely PIGGED OUT!

He ate throo one greezy,
wet paper bag,

one
glass
bottel,

one pyle
of dirt,

one
trakter
tyre,

one tree trunk,

and two misteryus brown lumps.

That nite the veree hungree caterpooper
got a stomack ache!

NO
WUNDA!

The next day was Sunday agen and
he cooldn't hold on one second longa.

He had to let go!

So he did!

It was lyke a volcayno!

He let go so much that he made a big,
new house...

a poocoon.

He stayed insyd his poocoon for moor than two weeks.

Then he nibbled his way out and...

He was a giant disgussting
dung-beetelee thing.

Afta that he got veree cross
becoz nobodee luved him.

So he took a
byt out of
the Erth...

he hed-butted
the moon...

...and he poot a massiv crack
in Uranus!

And nobodee lived happilee
eva afta except him.

The End.
Sweet Dreems, Sis!

And **THAT'S** how to make a
sweet little bedtime story

100 percent

UNBORING!

At last you've learned something!

Congratulations!

Now I bet you're itching to
send me lots and lots of cold hard cash
just as a way of thanking me for all my
free sample wisdom.

Well just

hold you're horses!

Because I'm not finished giving yet!

There's one last free
sample life lesson to come.

But first here's a short message from
another sponser who's not as good as
me, but is trying their best.

Oh, also there are some testimonials
saying how great I am that were NOT
written by me at all.

Never!

No way!

WHAT OTHERS ARE SAYING ABOUT MITEY MIKEY LIFE COACH FOR KIDS

'Yes, he's expensive but he's worth every cent!' Mr Smith's annoying son

'My life is soooo much better now that I'm nearly as smart as Mitey Mikey!' Mrs Browns crazy daughter

'Don't wait! Give him all your money now. What were you going to do with all that cash anyway?!' the weird kid who lives next door to the Lee's house

IT'S TIME FOR ANOTHER...

Everyone loves THE **Parental Attitude Adjuster**

brought to you by Crazy-Good STUFF Inc.

but have you ever **CONSIDERED** the incredible benefits of the MUTE BUTTON?

One click for fifteen minutes of attitude-free bliss!

ORDER NOW!

THE
Parental Attitude Adjuster

FROM

Crazy-Good STUFF Inc.

WITH THE ADDED BENEFITS OF **MUTE**

AND REMEMBER

It's not just good it's **CRAZY** good!

HEY! THAT'S ENOUGH ADS FOR USEFUL STUFF!

Let's get back to what really counts

ME!

Because I've got one last piece of free advice just for you.

Sometimes in our busy lives as kids we forget to simply relax. Then our minds fill with crazy thoughts and we go kind of nuts.

Unless, that is, we practice Mitey Mikey's super easy way to clear your mind completely.
This simple exercise will make your head as empty as your piggy bank after you've sent me all your money!

I call this . . .

Sample Life LESSoN #3:

Mindfoolness Coloring

All you have to do to empty your skull is color in lots of great pictures like this one.

I've done the first one so you can see how much of an expert I am.

Pretty good, huh.

But for mindfoolness to really kick in, you must say the right things while you color. So remember to follow the instructions on each page because, if you do, calmness will sink into your thick skull. Eventually.

(Oh and you can download all the color-in pages from sowrongbooks.com.
They're big-sized over there too, so go get 'em!
But only once you've finnished reading this book.
And not before!)

AS YOU COLOR SAY: I'm a perfect miracle made by the universe, just like the stars in the night sky. NOW SAY IT AGAIN!

COLOR AND SAY: I am floating on a river in the warm sunlight. The river is made of jello and the sunlight tastes like lemonade. Mmm, relaxing AND tasty. AGAIN!

COLOR AND SAY: I will become the best I can be by doing everything Mitey Mikey says - even if it costs me quite a lot of money. TEN MORE TIMES!

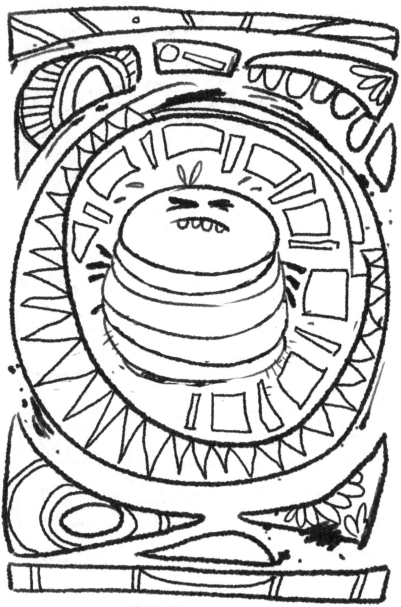

COLOR AND SAY:
Yes, Mitey Mikey is expensive but he's worth
every cent. SAY IT AGAIN AND AGAIN!

COLOR/DO: Breathe in and out and in and out and so on. Oh look, there's Uranus.

Whatever!
You've got the idea!

Well that's quite enough mindfoolness for now. If you want more you'll have to

PAY UP!

And to do that, just bust open your piggy bank and post all your money to

MITEY MIKEY
LIFE COACH FOR KIDS

And just think, soon you'll be nearly as amazing as me!

OK we're all done now!
This book is over!

Bye-bye!   Areevadierchi!

Sianara!   And over-and-out!

Because that's...

As well as cash payments, Mitey Mikey will accept:

- expensive gadgets
- pre-paid holidays for him and his baby sister
- vouchers for major theme parks (x2)
- houses
- land
- jewellery
- sports cars
- yachts
- and new pets

ABOUT THE AUTHOR

MICHAEL WAGNER WRITES BOOKS. BUT HE'S DONE OTHER THINGS TOO, LIKE . . .

GOT BORN

PLAYED WITH WATER

WENT TO SCHOOL

MADE A BAND

WORKED IN RADIO

GOT MARRIED

HAD A SON CALLED WIL

HAD A DAUGHTER CALLED LIZZIE

TAUGHT LIZZIE TO DRIVE

VISIT MICHAEL AT MICHAELWAGNER.COM.AU

ABOUT THE ILLUSTRATOR

WAYNE STARTED
DRAWING AT AN
EARLY AGE.

AND HE DIDN'T STOP.
HE DREW ALL DAY.

LOOK FOR WAYNE ONLINE.
HE'S OUT THERE SOMEWHERE.

If you thought
that was wrong,
you're wrong!

100% UNBORING GUARANTEED

So Wrong 2

EVEN WRONGER

Are you excited about
So Wrong 2, Sis?

Me too!

COLOR AND DO: Breathe in . . . now hold your breath and clench your muscles . . . now relax your muscles and breath in again! REPEAT!

SAY: If I don't give Mitey Mikey lots of money,
he might get angry like this guy. And we wouldn't
want that now would we! REPEAT!